Sá

CHRI

Book Two in the Sariah McDuff Series

by
Lee Ann Setzer

illustrated by
Robyn Officer

CFI
Springville, UT

Copyright © 2004 Lee Ann Setzer
All Rights Reserved.

No part of this book may be reproduced in any form whatsoever, whether by graphic, visual, electronic, film, microfilm, tape recording, or any other means, without prior written permission of the author, except in the case of brief passages embodied in critical reviews and articles.

ISBN: 1-55517-829-4
e.1

Published by Cedar Fort Inc.
www.cedarfort.com

Distributed by:

Edited by Janet Bernice
Cover Illustration by Robyn Officer
Cover design by Nicole Shaffer
Cover design © 2004 by Lyle Mortimer

Printed in the United States of America
10 9 8 7 6 5 4 3 2 1

Printed on acid-free paper

Library of Congress Cataloging-in-Publication Data

Setzer, Lee Ann.
  Sariah McDuff, Christmas detective / by Lee Ann Setzer.-- 1st ed.
     p. cm. -- (The Sariah McDuff series ; bk. 2)
  Summary: When Sariah learns that her best friend, Viola, will not have a Christmas tree or presents this year, she gathers clues and tries to discover how to give Viola her special Christmas wish--whatever that may be.
  [1. Christmas--Fiction. 2. Best friends--Fiction. 3. Friendship--Fiction. 4. Christian life-- Fiction. 5. Mystery and detective stories.] I. Title.

PZ7.S5125Sar 2004
[Fic]--dc22
                                          2004021295

CARDSTON & DISTRICT
PUBLIC LIBRARY

❄ SARIAH MCDUFF: ❄
❄ CHRISTMAS DETECTIVE ❄

DEDICATION

To my mom—
who has never given my children
a yodeling badger.

1
❄ DETECTIVES R US! ❄

My name is Sariah McDuff. I'm a detective. I prefer to work alone. My friend Viola Griswold also prefers to work alone. So we work together. She's the only person I know whose name is a musical instrument.

A detective needs a secret code, so Viola and I were working on ours.

"'A' should be a picture of an alligator," I said.

"No . . . too easy," said Viola. "How about an avocado?"

"I don't like avocados," I said. "How about Africa?"

Viola drew Africa. She frowned at it. "It looks like an upside down avocado," she said.

"Ok," I said. "Let's make 'B' stand for seventeen."

We made it up to "E," which was a picture of an eggplant. It looked a lot like an avocado, only right side up. Suddenly, something seemed wrong. I turned around in my chair and looked all around Viola's living room. I was right. Something was definitely wrong.

"Viola, why don't you have your Christmas tree up yet? We put ours up a week ago."

Viola said something that sounded like, "Roomph ermle groomp," but I couldn't be sure because she said it with her nose on her paper.

So I asked again. "When are you going to put up your tree?"

This time, Viola looked up. Her jaw was sticking waaayy out, and her eyebrows looked like they'd fallen off her forehead onto her eyelids. It was not a pretty sight.

She said much louder, "I said we're NOT having a tree."

Now, my eyebrows nearly shot off my head, somewhere into my bangs. "Not having a tree?"

"Crump erfer glermp," said Viola to her paper.

I wrote "F" on my paper, but I wasn't

thinking about secret codes anymore. I was thinking about Christmas trees. Specifically, I was thinking about Christmas trees that weren't there in Viola's living room. Suddenly, I dropped my pencil.

"Our first case!"

"What?" growled Viola with a terrible grumpy frown.

I picked up my pencil. "Er . . . nothing," I said. "Um . . . 'F' is for our first case, so I think 'F' ought to be the number one."

Viola looked at me out from under her very low eyebrows. "What first case?"

"Errrr . . . Any first case! As soon as we get one, that is. 'F' is for it."

Viola frowned at her paper. She wrote "F=1"

on it. "Murgle," she muttered.

Viola wasn't talking, except for "murgle," of course. It was clear that I was going to have to solve the Case of the Missing Christmas Tree on my own . . . and undercover.

By the time we reached the letter "M" which we decided would be one-half, (since "M" is one-half of the way through the alphabet), Sister Griswold was bringing us some drinks of water. It seemed like a good time to gather more Christmas tree clues.

"If you're not having a tree," I said, "where are you going to put your presents?"

Viola put down her water cup. Water splashed out on her paper and she said very, very clearly, "We're—not—having—presents—either!"

She said it so clearly I could have understood her if I'd been sitting in Manitoba instead of her living room. But since I was sitting in Viola's living room, I wiped a speck of Viola-spit off my earlobe.

We worked on our code until Viola frowned at her paper and said, "What should we do for 'T'?"

"Mmm," I said, pretending to think, "how about . . . a tree? Maybe a . . . Christmas tree?"

Viola put her knuckles on the table and leaned way over at me.

"Sariah," she said in a very grumbly voice, "if we keep talking about Christmas trees, I'm going to cry. And if you make me cry, I'm going to have to beat you up."

Viola is as big as a lot of fourth graders, and her knuckles were turning white, like they might start beating me up without Viola's permission.

So I stopped talking about Christmas trees . . . but I did not stop thinking about Christmas trees as I walked home in the snow, the secret code rustling in my pocket.

This case was hot, and it was up to me, Sariah McDuff, to solve it.

2
❅ THE "DO OPEN BEFORE ❅ CHRISTMAS" BOX

I wanted to ask my mom about the Griswolds and their missing Christmas, but when I got home, a bigger case was breaking.

I walked in the kitchen. The storm door slammed behind me.

"Look, Sariah! Grandma sent a box!" said my mom.

"Oh, boy!" I scrambled over to the table to see.

My big sister Margaret looked up from her

peanut butter sandwich. "Don't get too excited, Sariah," she said with her mouth full. "It's the 'Do Open Before Christmas' box."

I flopped down in a kitchen chair. "Nuts!"

Mom slit some tape on the box with a knife.

"Hey girls, that's no way to talk about gifts you haven't even seen yet!"

Margaret rolled her eyes. "It's the only way to talk about the 'Do Open Before Christmas' box, Mom."

I went to the counter and opened up the peanut butter.

"How come Grandma Smith always sends us such weird stuff, Mom?"

Mom sawed at some more tape. Both our

grandmas are expert tapers. She shrugged.

"Well, she loves you, and she loves to be silly. Christmas is the perfect opportunity for her to enjoy both the things she loves."

The last of the tape gave way. Mom pulled out crumpled newspaper. Margaret and I kind of edged over to the box, pretending like we didn't much care what was inside it.

Mom pulled out a squishy package with a tag that said, "For Margaret."

As she handed it to Margaret, the package started playing "Silent Night," sort of high-pitched and computery. Margaret looked at it like it might bite.

"Unwrap it, Margaret!" I said.

Margaret sighed and unwrapped it. "Oh,"

she said, holding a noisy pair of blue socks as far away from herself as her arm would reach.

"Silent Night" socks. The music was louder now that the socks were unwrapped. They had little stables with tiny little Marys, Josephs, and Baby Jesuses all over them.

"And for Sariah," Mom said, handing me a bigger package. It wasn't playing music, but it jingled. Margaret put down her socks to watch me.

The box kept jingling while I wrestled with Grandma's tape. When I finally got it open and looked inside, a stuffed reindeer was looking up at me.

"A stuffed animal?" I guessed. Usually Grandma Smith's gifts are much weirder than that. I pulled the reindeer out.

"A hat!" said Mom. "Put it on, Sariah, and let me take your picture!" Mom went to find the camera while Margaret and I stared at the hat. It was a knitted winter hat, and the stuffed reindeer's head was sticking out of the front. The jingles came from its antlers, which had dangly ornaments hanging off them. Mom appeared with the camera.

"Go ahead, put it on!" she urged. "You, too, Margaret."

The socks had stopped playing their song, but they started up again when Margaret picked them up. I put on the hat. It itched my ears, and the reindeer flopped down over my eyes.

"Margaret, sit on a chair and put your feet up so Grandma can see your socks," said Mom. "Smile for Grandma, girls!" We smiled. The camera flashed.

We took off our gifts—fast.

"Whew!" said Margaret, getting up to leave.

"Not so fast!" said Mom. "First you need to write your thank-you notes." She put sheets of paper in front of us.

Margaret sighed and found a pen. "What's a nice word for 'ugly,' Mom?"

"Try 'unique,'" said Mom from the kitchen. "And help Sariah spell 'interesting.'"

Margaret wrote for a minute. "There! How's this?

Dear Grandma, thank you for the very unique socks. They will look great! . . . She looked up . . . Under the bed.

"Now you need to say something about what a wonderful grandma she is."

Margaret and I finished our letters.

"Mom, can we put these away now?" asked Margaret.

Mom rolled her eyes. "If you must."

"Oh, believe me, Mom. We must!" I nodded as hard I as could to agree.

We marched upstairs to Margaret's bedroom. She got down on her stomach and pulled a box from waaaaaay out underneath her bed. We added our Grandma gifts. The socks lay there playing "Silent Night" to all the other

Do-Open-Before-Christmas gifts.

Margaret picked out a purplish little circle. "Remember the wreath made of dryer lint?"

"Yeah," I said, "and the yodeling badger?"

I squeezed a stuffed badger, and it howled out something that sounded like "Silent Night."

Sort of.

"Silent Night" is Grandma's specialty. I put the badger back in the box to keep the reindeer hat company. Then we shoved the box back under the bed.

Our first McDuff family Christmas tradition—airmail from Grandma—was complete.

3
❄ DANGER IS MY ❄ MIDDLE NAME

After dinner, Mom fitted me for my new Christmas dress. That meant standing perfectly still so Mom wouldn't poke me with pins. I stood on a box while Mom pinned with pins sticking out of her mouth. It seemed like a good time to collect more clues, since my mouth was really the only thing that could move.

"Mom, Viola says her family isn't having a Christmas tree or presents this year."

Mom looked up at me and made a noise like

what "oh" would sound like if you couldn't move your mouth because it was full of pins. "In fact," I went on, "I wonder if they're going to have Christmas at all. They're not playing Christmas music, or eating Christmas cookies, or . . . or . . . anything!"

Mom held up one finger like wait a minute, and did something under my arm with pins. I held even stiller.

"But, they can't just not have Christmas. That's not right, Mom!"

Mom finally finished using the pins she had in her mouth and tugged the bottom of the skirt for a minute. Then she looked up at me.

"I'd heard that Brother Griswold lost his job.

Maybe that's why they can't have Christmas this year."

I shook my head so hard I poked myself with one of the pins.

"No, Mom. Brother Griswold's job doesn't have anything to do with Christmas!"

"Money, Sariah," said Mom, reaching up to change a pin. "Maybe they don't have enough money to buy a tree and presents."

"But—!" She was on the neck now, behind me.

"You're right, Sariah. It's not right. What do you think we should do about it?"

"We?"

Mom helped me hop very carefully off the box. "Come upstairs to the mirror in my bedroom."

She helped me very carefully up the stairs. "What do you think?"

I stood in front of Mom's long mirror. "I think I can't move."

Mom frowned at the dress. "Could you move if it wasn't full of pins?"

I wiggled a little, and a pin tickled my backbone. "I think so."

I spun around on one toe. The red, sparkly skirt twirled around me. I grinned up at Mom.

"That about what you had in mind?" she asked.

I nodded.

"Okay, then change back into your clothes, and I'll show you something I got yesterday."

Mom helped me out of the pins, and I was so happy to be free that I bounced on her bed a couple of times. "Look at this, Sariah," Mom said.

She handed me a paper angel with a loop of ribbon tied to it.

"Seven-year-old girl, size ten," I read out loud. "What's this, Mom?"

"Well, Christmas Detective," she said, "I picked it off the 'Giving Tree' in Relief Society because I thought it sounded like Viola. Are there any other girls in your Primary class who are that big?"

"A clue!" I bounced on my bottom on her bed. "But, what's it for, Mom?"

"It's for helping out people who are having a hard time at Christmas. They write down what families might like for presents, then other families can help them get those things."

I turned the angel over. "It doesn't say what Viola wants for Christmas, though, Mom."

She nodded seriously. "That's why I need you to help me find out what she wants."

"Me?" I yelped. "She said she'd beat me up if I talked about Christmas any more!"

Mom's eyes got bigger for just a second, but then she said, real low and secret, "It's a dangerous undercover mission, Detective McDuff. Do you accept?"

I had to think about that one for a long minute. Finally, I nodded.

"Danger is my middle name, Mom. I accept."

I liked what Mom said, so I made a sign that said, "Sariah McDuff, Christmas Detective" and taped it to my bedroom door. That was the easy part. The hardest part was solving the case. I decided to start with my clues. I found a notebook with some blank pages.

"The Case of the Hidden Christmas Wish," I wrote.

"Clue Number One—Viola does not have a Christmas tree.

"Clue Number Two—You can't not have a Christmas tree.

"Clue Number Three—Ten dollars."

Ten dollars is how much Mom said we

could spend on this case.

"Of course!" I cried. Then I ran down the stairs.

"Mom!" I yelled, bursting through the kitchen door. "Let's get a Christmas tree for Viola! And decorations!"

Mom turned away from the sink where she was washing dishes and thought about that for a minute.

"A Christmas tree isn't really a gift, Sariah. Wouldn't you say it's more of a decoration?"

"But, Mom, they don't have one."

"Well, that's true enough."

Mom dried her hands and sat down at the table.

"You might not be able to get much of a tree,

though, for just ten dollars."

"Oh, ten dollars is a lot of money. And we'll get an angel for the top, and garlands, and balls!"

I raced back upstairs.

On my notes, I drew a beautiful Christmas tree. Then I wrote,

"Case Closed."

Clue 1–
Viola does not have
a Christmas tree.

Clue 2–
You can't not have
a Christmas tree!

Clue 3–
Ten dollars $

4
❄ WHAT'S THAT SMELL? ❄

The next day Viola and I were supposed to work on our spy gadgets, since I'd taken apart an old makeup case to get two mirrors we could use to make a periscope. I told Mom I'd case the joint. I already knew Viola's living room rug was green, but I couldn't remember what color the walls were, or how high the ceiling was.

But I knew right away something was different at the Griswolds' house when Viola opened the door. A strange smell came out.

I sniffed.

"What's that smell, Viola?" I asked, sniffing some more. "It smells like a pine tree."

"It is a pine tree, silly!" she said, very excited. "Come and see!"

Viola dragged me into the living room. Just standing in the doorway, I almost got poked by a huge Christmas tree on the other side of the room! It looked like it ought to be in a mall, or maybe an intersection.

"We had to cut it off just to get it in the door. See? Mom put the extra branches over the doors." Viola was right. Her living room looked like a forest.

"Um . . . I thought you weren't having a Christmas tree."

"My Uncle Bob works for this really rich guy who lives out in the country. He was putting up Christmas trees all over the guy's house, and this one was extra, so he brought it to us," Viola explained.

"Wow," I said.

My neck was getting sore from looking up at that tall thing. Then I noticed something else strange. That giant tree was covered with balls and garlands and pinecones and candy canes and bows and lights. It had a steeple thing on top that kind of leaned sideways because the tree was too tall for the ceiling.

"But, but . . . " I stammered, "Where did all those decorations come from?"

"The attic, silly. Do you want to string pop-corn?"

"I don't know. Is there room for it?"

Viola looked at me, very serious. "There is always room for more decorations on a Griswold Christmas tree."

Viola looked so much happier that I decided I might not get beaten up if I asked about Christ-mas presents.

"So," I said later as I tried to push a cranberry onto my needle, "what are you going to put under your tree?"

"Presents," said Viola. She didn't look like her face might fall off, like she had last time I asked, but her face definitely looked like she might have said, "spelling tests" or "dentist appointments," instead of "presents."

I put the eye-end of my needle on the table and pushed as hard as I could on that cranberry. It didn't move a bit. I tossed it back in the bowl and chose a piece of popcorn instead.

"You get presents! Great!"

Viola's spelling-test face slumped even further.

"My Aunt Bessie said she had an extra warm coat she could wrap up for me. Mom got erasers and lined paper on sale at J-Mart. And Santa's bringing underwear."

"Whoa! How do you know what Santa's bringing?"

"Mom said she talked to him."

I nodded. Moms pretty much know everything. I opened my mouth to ask why everyone was bringing boring presents, but Viola was getting that "I'll beat-you-up" look on her face again.

"Hey!" said Viola, "Let's put our strings together and see if we can make this string go all the way to the top of the tree!"

"Cool!" We tied the strings, then poked popcorn until we got a long, long string. Then Sister Griswold helped us get it to the top. The only way it reached that far was if we started at the bottom, then stretched it straight up to the top, like a bumpy white stripe.

We never did get around to making our periscope.

As I walked home, I thought about my new clues. Something didn't add up.

Underwear, even wrapped in reindeer wrapping paper, is not quite a Christmas present.

The right Christmas present for Viola wouldn't be boring—it would be exciting, and pretty, and shining.

"Of course!" I yelled out loud. Then I ran the rest of the way home.

Mom was in the sewing room, working on my Christmas dress. When I saw that big pile of sparkly red cloth and the package of white roses waiting to be sewn on, I stopped short.

Could I really do it?

Sariah McDuff, Christmas Detective, could solve any case, no matter how hard.

"Hi, Mom!" I said.

"Hi, Sariah," said Mom, without looking up. "I've just about got the sleeves on this."

Then she said something else—quiet so I couldn't hear it—probably a bad word, since she was sewing.

"Mom, I have a good idea!"

"That's great, honey." Mom still wasn't looking up, but I had to say it now, or I might not be able to say it at all.

"I think we . . .

"I think we should give my new dress to Viola."

The last part came out very fast, so I couldn't

change my mind.

Mom finally looked up. "Give your dress to Viola?"

"For Christmas. Because she wants something nice and not boring."

"So you want to give her this dress?"

Mom usually catches on faster than this.

"Yes, Mom! Please, can we? This way, it won't even cost ten dollars!"

Mom frowned.

"Well . . ." she said.

"Mom, Viola's been wearing the same dress to church since we were in first grade! It used to be way too long, but now it's way too short."

"Really?" said Mom. "I didn't know that."

"So, can we please, please give her my

Christmas dress?"

Mom held out an arm and I went over to get a hug. "That's really trying hard to be like Jesus, Sariah. I can't believe you'd give away your new dress."

"Me neither, Mom. But, can I?"

Mom sighed a big sigh.

"I'd love to let you, sweetheart." She held up the dress. "But, look at it. Do you remember that Viola's a size 10? You're a size 7. This dress wouldn't fit her."

"But . . ."

Mom shook her head sadly and put the dress down.

"If it were a little too small, I could fix it, but this one's a lot too small."

"But, what about making her one of her own? Then we could be twins!"

Mom shook her head again.

"Sorry, honey. Not enough fabric . . . and not enough time."

She stared across the room for a minute.

"Although, they might have something at the second-hand clothing store. You could get a lot there for ten dollars."

I waved my hands to erase that idea!

"No, Mom! She's already getting a coat that belonged to someone else!"

Mom blinked at me.

"Now, that's really being like Jesus, Sariah. You're trying to 'do unto others as you would have others do unto you.'"

I blinked back. "Um . . . what?"

"Treat other people like you'd like to be treated."

"Oh. Well, I wouldn't want a Christmas dress from the second-hand store!"

Mom smiled.

"Exactly! But now I'm afraid you're going to have to get right back on the Viola Griswold case and figure out something we can do."

I scuffled down to my room and got out my spy notebook.

I crossed out "Case Closed" and wrote, "Clue Number 4—Viola already has a Christmas tree."

Then I added, "Clue Number 5—And it is much bigger than ours."

"Clue Number 6—Viola has enough useful gifts already."

I chewed on my pencil.

Then I slapped it down on the desk.

Time to call in my sources on this one.

5
❄ ROCK'N'ROLL CHRISTMAS ❄

At dinner, I asked everybody what Viola might like.

"Well," said Mom, "it seems like you girls are always wearing through your socks and underwear. And you lose mittens and umbrellas and hats faster than I can buy them. What about a package of all those useful little things everyone needs? We could add toothpaste, and a little kit to fix her glasses, and—"

"No, Mom!" I cried, before she went any

farther. "Not underwear! Santa's bringing it, she said."

"Oh, ok," said Mom cheerfully. "Then what about some school supplies? There was a sale on erasers and lined paper, over at J-Mart—"

"Worse, Mom! No! It can't be useful. It has to be fun."

Mom looked at Dad. "Any ideas on fun, dear?"

"Well," said Dad, "when I was nine or so, this kid on my street was always taking his parents' sprinklers apart." He looked at us. "That was in California, where everyone had sprinklers. So, anyway, for his birthday his parents gave him his very own sprinkler to take apart and put together. It was keen! We must have taken the screws out of that thing fifty times. And there were a couple of ways you could put it back together, if you wanted a spaceship-looking thing, or a motorcycle kind of thing, without wheels, of course. Or—"

"Mom," Margaret interrupted, looking at Dad, "did you marry Dad on purpose?"

"Hm?" said Mom, also looking at Dad. "Yes, why?"

"Then why did you have to choose such a weird one?"

Margaret was in for it. Daddy took deadly aim with his fork and got her exactly in the nose with a blob of mashed potatoes.

"Dad!" shrieked Margaret.

Dad shrugged. "You started it, honey."

Margaret flicked off the mashed potatoes and leaned toward me. "Sariah, what if you got Viola some new clothes for her Fashion Girl doll? Those don't cost very much."

Margaret should know. She's thirteen, but I happen to know that she still plays with her Fashion Girl dolls sometimes.

I chewed my peas and swallowed before I said anything.

"Margaret, if we got Fashion Girl clothes for Viola, she would first have to find her Fashion Girls. One is up on the roof, under the snow. One is somewhere in the sandbox. One is in her dog's bed, and he growls at you if you come near it. And he chewed one leg off. Her other one is on the wall in the living room."

"The wall?"

I took a long drink of orange juice before I went on.

"Yes. Viola's little brother left a Fashion Girl, a bouncy ball, a 'kid's meal' race car, and three measuring spoons in the oven. It made a big blob thing. After the fire department left, the Griswolds cooled it off and hung it on the wall. Viola calls it a sculpture."

Margaret's fork fell to her plate while I was telling her this, and her mouth dropped open. "Sariah," she said, real low and serious, "do not ever buy that kid any Fashion Girl clothes!"

"Clue Number 7," I wrote after dinner, "sources are no help on this case."

Time was running out.

Christmas was only two weeks away, and still all I had were clues for what Viola would not like for a present. Then it finally happened—my first big break on the case.

Viola and I were in my living room with the Christmas tree, watching the "Girlz" show.

Suddenly, rock and roll Christmas music came on, with a close-up of Santa Claus's belt buckle rocking and rolling.

"Ooo! This is my favorite commercial!" Viola launched herself off the sofa and landed on her stomach in front of the TV.

"He's hip! He's hot! He's . . . Rock 'N' Roll Santa Claus!" yelled the TV guy.

Now you could see all of a toy Santa. A hand pushed a button, and Santa Claus started moving his hips and shaking his big stomach.

"Wow," I said. I've never seen this commercial before.

"Isn't he cool?" said Viola, while the TV guy talked about Santa's ten different tunes and three different dances. She pointed at the TV.

"That's what I want for Christmas, right there."

My eyes opened wider than wide.

"You do?"

But Viola was already staring at the TV again. She yelled, "Live! This Christmas!" with the TV man at the end of the commercial.

Rock 'N' Roll Santa had suddenly jumped

to the top of my suspect list. I needed more information.

"Girlz" started again.

"So," I said, casually collecting more clues, "how come you want a Rock 'N' Roll Santa for Christmas?"

Viola got back on the couch. "Because it's silly," she said. "It's not useful, and it won't last a long time, and I haven't been needing it for ages. It's just a silly Christmas thing."

Her shoulders turned slumpy.

"But I'm not gonna get him. I already know what I'm getting."

I suddenly noticed my mom standing in the living room doorway. Our eyes met, and we nodded at each other, very clever and sneaky.

After Viola left, Mom and I went straight to All-Mart. Rock 'N' Roll Santa was not hard to find. In fact, Rock 'N' Roll Santa was everywhere, with ladies who'd make him dance for you.

"He is kind of cute," Mom said when we saw him. She picked up a box and looked at the price tag.

"Uh oh."

I hopped up and down. "What, Mom? What?"

Mom shook her head and put the box back on the table.

"$29.99 is what, Sariah. It costs too much."

"But Mom," I cried, "we cracked the case! We caught the suspect! We solved the mystery! We can't turn back now!"

Mom got down on one knee next to me.

"I know, Sariah. I'm disappointed too." She scrunched up her face, like when she's thinking hard.

"We need a Plan B."

"Grmph," I grumped.

We stood and knelt there like that at All-Mart, her thinking and me grumping . . . for maybe three and a half minutes. Rock 'N' Roll Santa kept dancing and playing his Christmas tunes for all the other people. It sounded like he was making fun of us.

Finally Mom turned to me, very secret.

"I have an idea, Sariah," she said. Then she whispered, "Plan B."

She looked so excited and Christmassy that I bounced up and down. "What, Mom? What?"

She leaned in even closer. "Not here."

6
❄ VERY CHRISTMASSY! ❄

"We don't need that much tape, Sariah!"

"Yes, we do. It's a big box." I wound Scotch tape around the present Margaret and I were wrapping.

Mom laughed from the next room. "You can't fight it, Margaret. Sariah's a taper like her grandmothers before her!"

Margaret and I put five beautiful bows on the box while Mom called the Relief Society lady in charge of the Giving Tree. She came into the living room putting her coat on.

"It's all set, girls. She said we could take it over, but we have to do it in secret."

"Oh, boy!" I yelled.

Margaret didn't look so excited. "Are you sure about this, Mom?"

Mom smiled big. "Yep! Now get your coats on!"

We got in the car and drove to Viola's neighborhood in the dark, snowy night.

"She'll see the car tracks, Mom."

"Don't worry. We'll park a couple houses away."

Mom peered through the windshield.

"Which one is Viola's?"

"It has a sign with 'Welcome' spelled out in barbed wire."

"Oh . . . ok." Mom pulled up a few houses away. "I'll be waiting right here."

"Roger, Mom-lady," I said, pulling my coat up around my ears.

"Oh, brother," Margaret said.

We crept up sneakily, put the present on Viola's front porch, rang the doorbell, and ran like crazy. We jumped in the car and Mom peeled out of there.

"Cool!" said Margaret.

We didn't breathe again until we were safely on our own street.

"But, Mom," I asked, "how will we know if she likes it?"

In the dark, I could hear a smile in Mom's voice.

"Oh, I think we'll know."

The next Sunday, I was sitting in the Primary room, waiting for Sharing Time to start. Suddenly, over the noise of everyone talking, I thought I heard a sound. I turned around in my seat, so I was the first to see Viola walk in.

All at once, I recognized the sound. It was "Silent Night," the Christmas sock version. From her baby Jesus socks to the great big reindeer sticking out of her jingly hat, Viola was covered in Christmas! She walked slowly up the middle row, stopping to hold up her foot whenever someone looked to see where the music was coming from. And she kind of bounced when she walked, so everyone could hear the bells on her hat . . . and on her vest . . . also on her earrings, her necklace, and her shoelaces. In fact . . . you could hardly see her dress at all because of all the Christmas stuff. Before she sat down, she stood in front of everyone and pulled a little string on her Santa Claus necklace. Santa's red nose lit up, and everyone said, "Oooooo." Viola smiled and sat down.

Someone brushed my sleeve. I turned around, and it was Mom. She put one finger to her lips, like—shhh. I nodded, very sneaky.

Christmas detectives have to stay undercover.

Sharing Time that day was very Christmassy, because "Silent Night" was playing in the background pretty much the whole time. Sister Mikkelsen smiled at Viola and didn't say anything. Viola smiled back, waved, and flashed Santa's nose at her.

Everyone could hardly wait for class time with Brother Erkenbrack. Like he always does, he said, "Ok, does anyone have anything they'd like to tell us about?" Viola's hand shot in the air like a rocket. It jingled, of course, since she had three different reindeer bracelets on. "Yes, Viola?"

"Brother Erkenbrack, last night someone rang our doorbell, and when I opened the door, there was nothing there but this beautiful box!

And it said, 'DO open before Christmas!' So I did, and it was full of all this Christmas stuff!" She stood up and jingled all her bells at us. "Also a stuffed aardvark with an elf hat, and a plum pudding puppet, and an Advent calendar toaster cover, and . . . everything!" She did a little dance, and the socks played "Silent Night" like crazy.

Brother Erkenbrack smiled. "That's great, Viola. You look real Christmassy." Then he turned to the rest of us. "So, anybody else have something to share?" Everybody's hand went up.

"Parley?"

"Make Santa's nose go again, Viola!" said Parley, bouncing in his chair. Viola did.

"Zach?"

Zach walked up to Viola, kind of twitchy, like always, and stuck his nose up next to her earrings. He poked them with his finger, so they jingled. "Cool!" he said. Then he sat back down.

"Sariah?"

"Ummmm . . ." I always raise my hand, every week, but today I suddenly couldn't think of anything to say about the "Do Open Before Christmas" box. "Ummmm . . . can I try on your hat?" Viola skipped across the room, jingling, and plopped it on my head. I shook my head so the antlers rang, and everyone laughed. I almost started wishing I'd kept that hat, so I quick took it off my head and gave it back to Viola.

"Haynie?"

"How do those socks play 'Silent Night,' Viola?" asked Haynie, looking very close at Viola's ankles.

Viola took off her shoe and handed one of the socks to Haynie. "I can't tell," she said, "but it's in there somewhere." We all took a look, and everyone made a different guess about where the music came from.

Brother Erkenbrack cleared his throat, very loud. "Well, I guess if we're going to have a lesson, we'd better get started." Everyone looked at him.

"A lesson?" said Parley.

"Well, considering it's Primary and all . . . "

"Today?" said Haynie.

I don't remember what that lesson was about. But "Silent Night" was the background music.

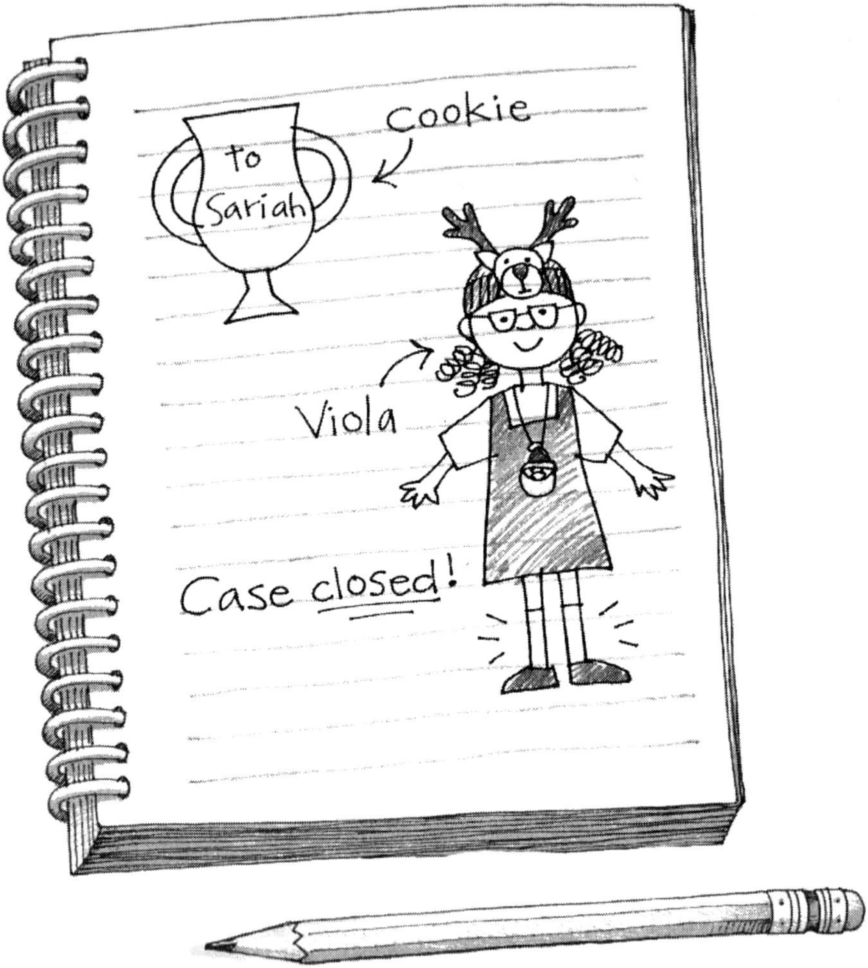
Cookie
to
Sariah
Viola
Case closed!

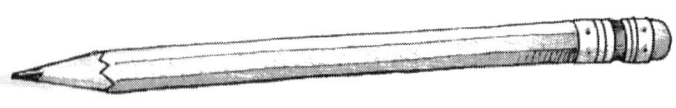

7
❄ CASE CLOSED ❄

Dad made Christmas cookies for us while we were at church. We were decorating cookies at the table and telling him about Viola and the "Do Open Before Christmas" box.

"But," Dad said, "what about sacrament meeting?"

Margaret shrugged. "The only 'Silent Night' we heard was on the organ."

"Viola told me," I said, "that her mom made her take all the Christmas stuff off and leave it in the car. But she put them back on after church!"

Dad chuckled. "Sounds like the 'Do Open Before Christmas' box was a big hit."

"Thank goodness it's gone!" said Margaret.

I nodded so hard agreeing that I could feel my eyeballs rattle.

"Remember what we talked about, when you wanted to give Viola your dress, Sariah?" asked Mom from the kitchen counter. "You followed Jesus, because you did for Viola what you would like someone else to do for you."

I suddenly coughed in the middle of a bite of cookie. Margaret handed me a napkin quick. When I could talk again, I cried, "No way, Mom! I would never, never, never want someone to give me the 'Do Open Before Christmas' box!"

Another, even more horrible thought came into my head. "Mom, what if someone did? What if someone decided we needed a new 'Do Open' box, because they were trying to be like Jesus?" Margaret looked a little scared, too.

Dad laughed. "Don't worry. There can't be two boxes like that in the world!"

"And," said Mom, quick before I could say anything else, "Jesus didn't say anything about the 'Do Open' box. The trick about 'do unto others' is that you have to do for them what you would want them to do for you, if they were you."

"Even some grownups never manage it," said Dad.

I scrunched up my eyebrows to help me

think. "I don't think I can fit all those 'do untos' into my head at the same time, Mom. And we didn't even spend any money."

"Would Viola have been any happier if we'd spent ten dollars on underwear or Fashion Girl clothes?" asked Mom.

"Hm," I said at the same time Margaret gasped, "Don't say that, Mom!"

"Guess what?" said Mom. "Spending money is easy. Cracking a hard case is hard. And you did it!"

Mom brought over the cookie tray she'd been working on at the counter. My mouth dropped open. Mom gave me a hug.

"You are, in fact, one tough cookie!"

On the tray was a giant cookie shaped like

a big trophy and frosted yellow. In frosting, it said:

Awarded to
Sariah McDuff—
Christmas Detective,
for Solving the Case of the
Hidden Christmas Wish!

That night, I drew a picture of Viola in her reindeer hat in my spy notebook.

Then I drew a picture of my cookie trophy.

"Case Closed," I wrote.

CARDSTON AND DISTRICT
PUBLIC LIBRARY

3 1817 01151 7117

❄ ABOUT THE AUTHOR ❄

Lee Ann Setzer likes to talk with children. She is a speech therapist by profession and a mother of three, so she gets plenty of practice. She lives with her family in Springville, Utah.

Gathered: A Novel of Ruth, is Lee Ann's first book. *Sariah McDuff: Primary Program Diva* is the first in the *Sariah McDuff* series.

Look for these fine books in your favorite bookstore, or order them at www.cedarfort.com

9 26575 78294 6

DEC 0 3 2004